The Fox and the Crow

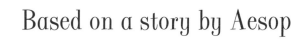

Based on a story by Aesop

Retold by Rosie Dickins

Illustrated by Rocío Martínez

It was a warm
summer's day
and Fox was
feeling hungry.

"The bees have honey,"
he sighed.
"Rabbit has a carrot.
What is there for me?"

Then, he smelled something delicious.
He looked up, licking his lips.

High in the
treetops sat Crow...

...with a big chunk of
crumbly yellow cheese.

Fox closed his eyes and sniffed longingly.
But the cheese was far out of reach.

Mmmm...

"What can I do?"
He gave a crafty smile.

"Ahem!"
Fox cleared
his throat.

"Oh beautiful Crow!"
he began.

Crow looked down, startled.

No one had ever
called her **beautiful** before.

"What sleek, shining feathers you have! What a fine midnight black they are!"

Crow's beak was too full to reply.
But she fluttered her wings proudly.

"Yes, yes,"
she thought,
eager to
hear more.

"Is your singing voice as beautiful as your feathers?" sighed Fox.

I wish you would sing to me.

Crow hopped
shyly from foot
to foot.

"Please sing," begged Fox.

Go on!

"Just a note,"
he pleaded.
"For me?"

Crow couldn't resist.

She stretched her beak wide and screeched.

Caw! Caw!

Down tumbled the cheese...

SNAP!

...straight into Fox's
waiting jaws.

Give it back!

Crow flapped furiously.

"Hey!" she snapped.
"That is MY cheese!"

Fox gulped it down and gave a broad, cheesy grin.

"Not any more," he laughed.

That was delicious!

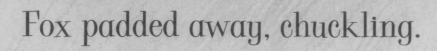

Fox padded away, chuckling.

Crow was cross...

but she had learned
her lesson – don't be
fooled by flattery.

About the story

People think this story was written about 2,500 years ago
by a man named Aesop. He told many stories about animals,
always ending with a 'moral' or lesson about how to behave.

Edited by Lesley Sims
Designed by Laura Wood
Additional design by Non Figg and Louise Bartlett

This edition first published in 2014 by Usborne Publishing Ltd., Usborne House,
83-85 Saffron Hill, London EC1N 8RT, England. www.usborne.com
Copyright © 2014 Usborne Publishing Ltd.